THE SUPREME DREAM MACHINE

Books by the same author

The Hell Hound of Hooley Street
Little Stupendo

Picture Books
You're a Hero, Daley B

THE SUPREME DREAM MACHINE

JON BLAKE

Illustrations by

PAUL SAMPLE

WALKER BOOKS
AND SUBSIDIARIES
LONDON • BOSTON • SYDNEY

First published 1998 by Walker Books Ltd
87 Vauxhall Walk, London SE11 5HJ

2 4 6 8 10 9 7 5 3 1

Text © 1998 Jon Blake
Illustrations © 1998 Paul Sample

The right of Jon Blake to be identified as author
of this work has been asserted by him in accordance with the
Copyright, Designs and Patents Act 1988.

This book has been typeset in Plantin.

Printed in England

British Library Cataloguing in Publication Data
A catalogue record for this book
is available from the British Library.

ISBN 0-7445-4181-6

Contents

Contents

Chapter 1

My Little Shop and Parent Problems

It was the summer holidays, and on our garden gate I put a sign: LIAM'S BYGONES. Behind that was an old desk, and on the desk were:

three plastic razors (used)
an interesting jamjar
one paintbrush
a china cat (one ear)
postcards from Dublin, Majorca and the
    Isle of Wight
a pair of clogs from Amsterdam
a spoon engraved with the words:
    University of Liverpool
seven bottles of *Blue Lagoony.*

Blue Lagoony was my pride and joy. It was a perfume which I had made myself. The exact recipe is, of course, a secret, but the instructions go something like this:

1. Choose a selection of rose petals and place in a jar.
2. Add a few sprigs of honeysuckle.
3. Cover with water, add a teaspoonful of sugar and some secret ingredients.
4. Leave to stand for three days then pour through a tea strainer into another jar or bottle.
5. Scrape any scum or mould off the mixture with your finger.
6. Label and leave in a cool place for a further week.

I still hadn't got it quite right. It always seemed to come out a muddy brown colour. The smell wasn't too wonderful either, a bit like bad drains. Dad suggested I call it *Brown Puddle* or *Eau de Toilet.* But I knew *someone* out there would buy it. Someone with a bad cold, for example, who had lost their sense of smell.

Unfortunately, a week had passed, and that special someone still hadn't shown up. In fact, to be honest, I hadn't actually sold anything. My sandwich-box safe still had the same twenty pence I put there on Saturday. My friends were all laughing at me and telling me what fun they'd had at Beany Castle Theme Park. But I wasn't giving up easily.

Then, at last, a customer came to the shop. Well, not exactly a customer. More like my mum.

"Liam," she said, "we're very worried about you."

"Why?" I said. "What's the matter with me?"

"You're a young person," she said. "You should be out running around, not sitting here behind this ... nonsense." Mum swept her hand over my little counter and the things I'd carefully laid out, and the signs I'd made. "Anyway," she added, "you're making the place look untidy."

Ha! So that was the real problem. In that case I *definitely* wasn't moving.

"I'll tidy it away in two weeks," I said.

Mum went inside for reinforcements. Ten minutes later, Dad came out.

"Pack your bags," he said. "You're going on holiday."

Chapter 2

Uncle Hector, Uncle Hodge and the Potato Family

I was already in the car and halfway out of town when I realized I had no idea where I was going.

"You're staying with your uncles," said Mum.

"Which uncles?" I asked.

"Uncle Hector," said Dad, "and Uncle Hodge."

"Hector and Hodge?" I sneered. "I've never heard of them!"

"They're not your real uncles," said Mum. "They're your second-uncles-twice-removed-by-marriage."

"Why are they looking after me?" I asked.

"We're paying them," replied Dad.

"Are they fun?" I asked.

The car instantly filled with laughter.

"Hector and Hodge," said Mum, "are probably the dullest people in the world."

"As far as we know," said Dad, "they haven't been out of doors for ten years."

"That," added Mum, "is why we're sending you to them."

Suddenly it all became clear to me. The purpose of this holiday was to teach me a lesson. After two weeks with my boring uncles, I would be gagging for skateboards and beach-balls and Beany Castle Theme Park. My shopkeeping days would be over.

Well, I thought to myself, we would see about that!

We drove into a village called Chipping Dollop. It was as quiet as the grave. There was a post office, a church and a lazy old dog scratching its ear. We pulled up outside a flat grey cottage with tiny windows and a small garden of weeds.

"Knock on the door," said Mum. "They'll be expecting you."

I climbed out of the car and with a great heave yanked my suitcase after me. I'd packed pyjamas, toothbrush, change of undies and about fifty jars of *Blue Lagoony*.

Dad sped away. Putting a brave face on things, I did as I was told and rapped the old iron door-knocker.

There was a long silence, then the sound of slowly shuffling slippers. The door opened and there stood a little pale man with a faint moustache and small lifeless eyes. His thin white neck disappeared into a hard white collar which was several sizes too big for him. For a moment I thought he might sink into his suit like a tortoise into its shell.

"Hello," I said. "I'm Liam."

The little pale man gave a weak grunt, then turned his back and walked into the house. I followed him down a dim passage past a grandfather clock stuck at five past twelve. I arrived in a room like a museum, with cold brown furniture, a faded picture of a faithful hound and two armchairs. The pale man sat down in one of them. Opposite him, in the other chair, was a very disturbing man indeed. He looked like a waxwork, with wild grey hair and even wilder grey eyebrows which spilled over his glasses like trailing plants. But the worst thing about him was the huge toothy smile which seemed stuck on his face. I knew right away that this was my Uncle Hector.

"Turned out nice again," he said unexpectedly.

"What, the weather?" I asked.

"The upside-down pudding," replied Uncle Hector. He put back his fixed smile and that was the end of the conversation.

Half an hour passed. Nothing happened.

Another half hour passed. Even less happened.

I decided I'd better break the silence. "Is there anything for me to do?" I asked.

A small frown appeared between Uncle Hector's eyebrows, though his smile stayed exactly the same.

"Anything to do?" he repeated.

"Like a game," I suggested.

"A game?" repeated Uncle Hector.

Uncle Hector puzzled over this for a while, then seemed to have an idea.

"Hodge," he ordered, "fetch the Potato Family."

Uncle Hodge went out and came back with four potatoes, which he placed in front of me.

"I don't think I know this game," I said.

"It's very simple," said Uncle Hector. "The two big ones are Mummy and Daddy Potato, and the two little ones are the children."

"How do you play?" I asked doubtfully.

"That," said Uncle Hector, "is entirely up to you."

I did my best to play with the Potato Family. Mummy and Daddy had a fight, then the little girl got lost, then the little boy had to go to the doctor with a worm in his head.

After that they all sat down and watched telly and I looked around for something else to do.

"Have you got a garden?" I asked.

The two uncles scratched their heads and tried to remember.

"There *was* a garden," said Uncle Hector, "last time I looked."

"Can I play in it?" I asked.

"Why?" asked Uncle Hector, puzzled.

"It might be fun," I replied.

"Fun?" repeated Uncle Hector. His eyes roved round the room a few times while he tried to make sense of this unusual word.

"Can I?" I pleaded.

"Very well," said Uncle Hector. "But be careful of things falling from the sky."

Uncle Hector had definitely been indoors too long.

Chapter 3

A Garage Full of Junk and an Excellent Idea

I was not surprised to find that the back garden was a jungle. I half expected Tarzan to come swinging out of it. I thought about playing Tarzan myself, except I didn't fancy falling into fifty thousand nettles.

On the other side of the house there was a gravel path. At the end of this was a ramshackle old garage made of red iron sheets. I decided to take a peek inside.

The garage was chock full of junk. I began climbing through it, making a list of what I found:

one old tin bath
one stuffed owl in a glass case
two empty rabbit hutches
one broken gas fire
a motor bike helmet (ancient)

several planks of wood (various sizes)
one mouldy suitcase
one rickety wall-papering table
seven sweetie jars filled with nuts, bolts,
   etc.
one massive spider, possibly a tarantula
one armchair (no springs or seat, otherwise
   perfect).

Suddenly I had a brilliant idea. This could
be my new shop! Not just a shop, a
superstore!

I set to work straight away. I used the
rickety wall-papering table for a counter, and
put the motor bike helmet and stuffed owl on
it. The mouldy suitcase went underneath.
That was my safe for all the money I was
going to make.

Next I found some paints and made a sign
saying: SHOP OPEN. I put the sign at the top
of the drive, then went indoors to ask
permission to do all the things I'd already
done. Unfortunately both my uncles were

fast asleep, and I didn't like to wake them, so I just went back out, selected a long plank, and started painting another sign to go over the door.

I decided to call the shop TWO UNCLES GENERAL STORES. One day, Two Uncles would be a name as well known as Tesco's or Marks & Spencer. Then my friends wouldn't laugh.

Just as I was finishing this sign, I had a strange feeling that I was being watched. I turned quickly, just in time to see Uncle Hodge shrinking back hurriedly from a window.

I propped up the sign and carried on clearing out the garage.

Uncle Hector's face appeared at the window. Uncle Hodge hovered behind him. I waved and carried on.

Chapter 4

The Old Enfield and a Gleam of Life

....

The back door opened. The two uncles
emerged, blinking in the bright daylight.
Uncle Hector led the way, head down, eyes
everywhere, like a creeping tomcat. Uncle
Hodge pottered nervously behind, his head
popping up and down over Uncle Hector's
shoulder. Slowly they homed in on me.

"Hello," I said. "I'm making a shop."

Uncle Hector ran his eyes over the counter
where I had now displayed one jar of *Blue
Lagoony* and most of the contents of his
garage. Then he peered past me. Something
inside was interesting him.

In the far corner of the garage was
something big and bulky covered in a canvas
sheet. I hadn't explored it because I was
afraid it was a dead body or a sleeping bear.
But it was this which fascinated Uncle

Hector. He crept towards it and sniffed the air like a mouse after cheese. Except there wasn't any smell of cheese – just a slight scent of engine oil.

Suddenly, like a conjuror, Uncle Hector whipped off the canvas sheet. There stood the most incredible motor bike, as ancient as the pyramids, with seats like horse saddles and an engine like a ship's boiler room on wheels.

A flicker of life came to Uncle Hector's eyes. He seemed to be struggling with some dim memory. Meanwhile, a happy, rather childish smile had crept on to Uncle Hodge's face.

"The ... old ... Enfield!" he mumbled.

Uncle Hodge edged past Uncle Hector and began giving the old bike little gentle strokes as if he were fondling a kitten.

"Shall we get it out?" I asked. I was already picturing the bike at the front of my shop with "Star Offer" written on it.

It took all three of us to wheel the old

Enfield out into the light. It smelled of world wars and distant summers, lost loves and sooty factories. We were wheeling out history.

Rather uncertainly, Uncle Hector climbed aboard.

"I wonder if it still works?" he mused aloud.

Uncle Hector rammed down the kickstart.

Once ... twice ... then WROOOOOOM! The throaty roar filled the whole street. And at the same time that the old bike came to life so a dangerous gleam came into Uncle Hector's eyes. It was as if the kickstart had brought *him* to life as well. I can't really describe how different he had become, but if you wave a piece of raw liver beneath a sleeping cat's nose you may get some idea.

Uncle Hector wasn't the only one to come alive. The engine had a magical effect on Hodge as well. He began gabbling breathlessly, reminding Hector of the time they travelled here and there, the picnics, the adventures, the night-time flights into the unknown, on and on and on like a burst balloon letting out twelve years' worth of air.

Uncle Hector wasn't really listening. With a swift check of the hand-controls, he put the bike into gear, flew forward ten metres and pitched head-first into the nettles.

"Uncle Hector!" I cried. "Are you all right?"

Uncle Hector struggled to his feet. He didn't seem to notice the nettle stings. The gleam in his eyes was hotter than the sun.

"Get the helmets," he said. "Let's burn rubber!"

Chapter 5

The Sidecar and a Visit to Town

....

Soon Uncle Hector had made plans for a trip to town. This put me in a difficult position. I still hadn't counted and listed the nuts and bolts in the seven sweetie jars. Should I stay and do my duty, or should I go for a spine-tingling white-knuckle ride on a legendary motor bike?

Uncle Hector soon made up my mind for me. He handed me a crash helmet and plonked a sign on the counter saying:

CLOSED

EVEN FOR MASHEMS TEA.

However, there was still one small problem. The old Enfield only had two seats, and there were three of us.

Uncle Hector wasn't going to let this stop us. He soon had a solution.

"Young Liam can ride on the back seat," he

said, "and Hodge can go in the sidecar."

"Sidecar?" I replied. "What sidecar?"

Uncle Hector took me quietly to one side. "You may have noticed," he whispered, "that Hodge is not quite *all there*."

We both glanced over at Uncle Hodge who was happily making friends with a bumble-bee.

"Yes," I replied. "I had noticed."

"If we *tell* him there's a sidecar," continued Uncle Hector, "he'll believe there *is* a sidecar."

"Ah," I said.

Without further ado Uncle Hector went and explained to Uncle Hodge. Uncle Hector's arm pointed dramatically at the space beside the bike, while Uncle Hodge scratched his head and felt about in the air with an uncertain expression.

I can't say I felt comfortable about playing this trick. It didn't seem right, or fair, or very nice. But it was difficult to say no to Uncle Hector now that he promised so much fun.

We climbed up on to the bike. Uncle Hodge shuffled up alongside, still scratching his head.

"That's it, Hodge," said Uncle Hector. "In you get."

Tentatively, Uncle Hodge opened an imaginary door and squatted down on to an invisible seat.

"All aboard!" said Uncle Hector. "Let's go!"

Uncle Hector rammed the kickstart, revved the bike, and shot off, with me hanging on for dear life and Uncle Hodge still squatting on the driveway behind us.

Uncle Hector braked. "No, no, no, Hodge!" he called. "It's not an automatic sidecar! It's a *run-along* sidecar! You have to move it yourself!"

Uncle Hodge hesitantly began a kind of squatty duck-walk up the drive.

"That's better!" said Uncle Hector. "Now faster!"

Uncle Hodge speeded up his duck-walk.

Uncle Hector revved the bike. Uncle Hodge pursued us like a frantic cossack dancer.

The moment the bike set off, Uncle Hodge realized his only chance of keeping up was to stand up and run like blazes. For someone who'd been indoors for twelve years, he was surprisingly fit. However, he didn't look particularly happy, and now and then seemed to be shouting at Uncle Hector in protest. But you could only see his mouth opening and closing because of the great throaty roar of the old Enfield.

It was a fantastic feeling, sitting up on that great leather saddle, roaring majestically through the countryside. The old Enfield seemed to have a personality of its own, and I could almost imagine it with eyes and teeth like a motor bike in a kiddy's picture book.

At last, however, we reached Uglington, which I recognized because of the Superbowl, the Laserdome and the Rio Monster Ten-Screen Cinema. Uncle Hector, on the other hand, didn't recognize a thing. Town had changed a lot in the last twelve years.

Uncle Hector decided to pull up and check his map. Uncle Hodge gradually caught up with us, looking very red and letting out great wheezes of dusty breath.

"Ah!" said Uncle Hector, stabbing his finger into the map. "*This* is where we will go!"

"Where is that?" I asked.

"Jim Doobrey's Motor Cycle and Sidecar Emporium!" replied Uncle Hector.

Uncle Hodge enthusiastically agreed, no doubt hoping we might buy a more comfortable sidecar.

Uncle Hector turned to me with glee in his eyes. "Now Liam," he said, "you will see a *real* shop!"

Chapter 6

The Future Machine and a Large Amount of Money

··

When we arrived at the chosen spot on the map, however, Uncle Hector was in for a shock. Jim Doobrey's Motor Cycle and Sidecar Emporium was no more. In its place was a monster superstore called Rev City.

Uncle Hector gave a great huff. "Call this a motor bike shop?" His lip curled scornfully. "It's more like a ... a giant shoebox!"

This seemed a strange comparison but I couldn't think of a better one. Rev City may have been big but it had no character at all.

"I expect it's got lots of bikes," I said helpfully.

"Yes," said Uncle Hector, "and not one to match the old Enfield."

Uncle Hector gave the old Enfield an

affectionate slap, and Uncle Hodge did the same to the imaginary sidecar. We wandered up to the windows of Rev City.

"Call this progress?" sneered Uncle Hector. "Call this the future? Call this..."

Uncle Hector's voice trailed off and he became completely silent. I noticed that his eyes were growing big and round. I followed his gaze towards the most sensational two-wheeled machine you could ever imagine. Its seat was like an armchair and its engine was like a power station. Above it hung a sign:

FARLEY-DAVIDSON FUTURE

MACHINE

THE MOST ADVANCED TWO-

WHEELED VEHICLE IN THE WORLD.

Suddenly the old Enfield looked like a donkey.

"It's wicked!" I said.

"I want it," said Uncle Hector.

We soon realized that Uncle Hector meant

what he said. Without another word he marched into the shop and a few seconds later appeared on the other side of the window, right next to the Future Machine, as if he was already its proud owner.

A salesman appeared from nowhere and homed in on Uncle Hector. He was a short dumpy man with a sad grey face and a shiny blue suit. On his badge it said: MR MERRIMAN, JUNIOR SALES ASSISTANT. Uncle Hector asked him an urgent question, Mr Merriman gave a lazy answer, and Uncle Hector's face suddenly dropped.

"I think he asked him the price," I said to Uncle Hodge.

I was right. Mr Merriman picked up a card which had fallen off the Future Machine. I can't remember the exact price, but it looked like a pretty good pinball score.

Uncle Hector floated sadly away, like a deflated balloon. We met him at the door.

"I had my heart set on that," he said.

"Never mind," I replied. "We've still got

the old Enfield."

Uncle Hector looked up at the bike as if he had forgotten all about it.

"That?" he said. "That pile of old junk?"

Uncle Hodge gasped at this terrible insult. His lips juddered as if he was desperate to protest, but nothing came out.

Meanwhile, a sign above the door had come to Uncle Hector's attention:

REV CITY PRICE GUARANTEE
IF YOU FIND ANY BIKE CHEAPER IN
ANOTHER SHOP, WE WILL MATCH
THEIR PRICE

Uncle Hector's brain began to whirr.

"I *will* have that bike yet!" he muttered.

Chapter 7

Uncle Hector's Great Plan

Back at the house, Uncle Hector paced about, thinking hard. Several times he came out into the backyard to watch me setting out the Two Uncles General Stores. As he watched he hummed and ha'd and stroked his chin. He wasn't this interested in the shop before, I thought to myself.

Eventually Uncle Hector called us together for a meeting. He began walking in a circle with his hands behind his back, which is how clever people walk. I followed him, doing the same. Uncle Hodge followed me, still puffing and panting from his ride in the imaginary sidecar.

"Gentlemen," said Uncle Hector, "I have a plan."

"Go on," I said.

"They say that if we can find the bike cheaper in any shop, they will match the price," said Uncle Hector.

"That's right," I said.

Uncle Hector's arm swept dramatically in the direction of the Two Uncles General Stores. "*This* is a shop," he said.

I agreed.

"So if we put a Farley-Davidson here, and make up a stupid price for it, they'll have to sell us their bike for the same price!"

"Hmm," I said doubtfully. "What kind of stupid price were you thinking of?"

"Ten pence," suggested Uncle Hector.

"Ten pence?" I repeated, even more doubtfully.

"Ten pence," confirmed Uncle Hector.

Uncle Hector was obviously mad, but it did seem to be a brilliant plan.

Apart from one small thing.

"We haven't *got* a Farley-Davidson to put in the shop," I said.

"No," agreed Uncle Hector, "that's the only problem."

"And it would cost us fifteen thousand

pounds to buy one," I added.

"Unless we borrow one," said Uncle Hector.

"Who from?" I asked.

Uncle Hector hesitated for a moment. "I know where we *might* find one," he said. "But it could be rather ... dangerous."

A tingle of fear went down my spine.

"Tell us more," I said.

"There was a group of bikers who used to meet up in Chipping Valley," said Uncle Hector. "Wild, frightening people."

The tingle went back up my spine. "What were they called?" I asked.

"Hell's Nurses," replied Uncle Hector.

"Hell's Nurses?" I gasped.

"Many years ago they were just ordinary nurses," continued Uncle Hector, "but they got fed up with being helpful and nice *all* the time. So they dressed up wild, and bought these bikes, and ... and..."

Uncle Hector was too frightened to go on.

"Maybe we should forget this idea," I said.

"Maybe," agreed Uncle Hector. "But I had my heart set on taking you to school next term."

"On the Future Machine?" I asked.

"Exactly," replied Uncle Hector.

I pictured myself cruising into the playground. I pictured the faces of my friends.

"Where did you say we'd find these Hell's Nurses?" I asked.

Chapter 8

Chief Sister Nursie Meets the Blue Lagoony

....

That evening, armed with a jar of *Blue Lagoony*, I set off for Chipping Valley. If there was any trouble, I would not hesitate to open the jar and release the disgusting stink. Even so, my legs were like jelly and my heart was racing faster than the old Enfield at full throttle. As I reached the valley, the sun had set and a shivery darkness was everywhere. I huddled up behind a tree and looked down.

No one could imagine the sight beneath me. A dozen mighty bonfires lit up the valley, with a hog roasting on each. Fifty roaring bikes raced up and down beside a wild rushing river. Each bike was ridden by a Florence Nightingale gone badly wrong. Their nurses' pinnies were worn beneath studded leather jackets, with fearsome black boots beneath. Their little caps were perched upon terrible helmets with great cattle horns sticking up on either side. They whirled stethoscopes and bedpans above their heads and let out blood-curdling cries of war.

One of the nurses lined up her bike facing the river and revved up. Suddenly she started racing full tilt straight at it. The bike took off, sailed over the stream and skidded to a halt on the other side. The others revved and wheelied and generally showed their appreciation. Then the biggest, fiercest nurse of all rode up to the rider and pinned something to her.

"Hail Kelly-Marie!" roared the big nurse. "Hail the newest of our number!"

"Hail Chief Sister Nursie!" replied Kelly-Marie. "Where you lead, so shall I follow!"

There was a cheer. At that moment my eyes caught sight of the huge metal stallion Chief Sister Nursie sat upon. It couldn't be ... it was! A Farley-Davidson Future Machine!

I was so excited, the jar of *Blue Lagoony*

dropped clean out of my hands ... rolled down the hill ... and landed with a *clunk* against the big black boots of Chief Sister Nursie.

Chief Sister Nursie picked up the jar and inspected the label I had so carefully written.

"Perfume!" she roared.

As one, the nurses spat on the ground.

"Who dares to send us *perfume*!" demanded Chief Sister Nursie.

Chief Sister Nursie's eyes followed the trail of the *Blue Lagoony* back up the side of the valley. She gave orders to the others, and suddenly bikes were coming towards me from all sides. I shook so much the leaves fluttered from my tree. They spotted me in an instant, and the next second I was in the iron grip of arms which smelled of engine oil and TCP. They slung me across the back of a bike and brought me back in triumph to Chief Sister Nursie.

"What is the meaning of this?" she barked, holding the *Blue Lagoony* to my face.

"Um..." I said. "Er..."

"We hate perfume!" said Chief Sister Nursie. "Perfume makes us *sick*!"

"Actually," I said helpfully, "this perfume makes *everybody* sick."

"Pah!" said Chief Sister Nursie. "I'll show you what we do with perfume!"

Chief Sister Nursie began to unscrew the lid of the jar.

I held my breath.

Chief Sister Nursie removed the lid.

The entire valley was drenched in the stink of mould, marmalade and foul stenching drains.

A look of surprise came over Chief Sister Nursie's face, followed by the warmest of smiles. "Mmmmm!" she purred.

"Mmmmm!" purred the others.

I looked about me. Some of the nurses had their eyes closed as if in a pleasant dream. Others were taking deep lungfuls of breath. One or two had even dropped off their bikes and were rolling around in delight.

"We must have this perfume!" cried Chief Sister Nursie. She began lashing great handfuls of it over her neck, leaving faint brown stains and an ungodly stench.

"Are you sure?" I said.

"How much?" demanded Chief Sister Nursie. "We'll give you anything!"

My eyes fell on the monstrous machine beneath Chief Sister Nursie's bum.

"All right," I said coolly. "I'll do you a deal."

"Go on," said Chief Sister Nursie.

"If I can have your bike for *one day*," I said, "you can have this bottle of perfume and a dozen more besides."

Chief Sister Nursie laughed. "My Future Machine?" she said. "You think I'd trust a whippersnapper like you with my Future Machine?"

I grabbed the *Blue Lagoony*. I was getting confident. "Forget the perfume then," I said, turning to go.

"Wait!" cried Chief Sister Nursie.

The Hell's Nurses went into a huddle. After a brief discussion, Chief Sister Nursie turned back to me.

"Very well," said Chief Sister Nursie. "You may have the Future Machine. On one condition."

"Go ahead," I said.

Chief Sister Nursie came right up to me, nose to nose. "If I don't get my bike back on time and in perfect order," she said, "we will operate on you."

"Operate?" I repeated nervously.

"Yes!" replied Chief Sister Nursie gleefully. "Why should doctors and surgeons have all the fun? Why shouldn't nurses open people up once in a while?"

The rest of the nurses howled in agreement. I looked down at my precious little body and swallowed hard.

"Very well," I said.

Chapter 9

Uncle Hodge Takes Charge

....

It was the proudest moment of my life as I wheeled the Farley-Davidson Future Machine up the drive of my uncles' house. Uncle Hector rushed out to greet me like a long-lost son, and I told the story of Chief Sister Nursie and the *Blue Lagoony* without stopping for a single breath. I added a few bits, like how I jumped through the ring of fire on the motor bike, but I mainly told the truth. Now it was time to put the Great Plan into action. Uncle Hector called out Uncle Hodge to help him make some space in the Two Uncles General Stores.

Meanwhile, I made the sign:

FARLEY-DAVIDSON FUTURE MACHINE

THE MOST ADVANCED TWO-WHEELED

VEHICLE IN THE WORLD

10P.

We wheeled the bike into place. It fitted snugly between the old tin bath and the broken armchair. The effect was electric. No longer did I have a dusty old corner shop. The Two Uncles General Stores had become a superstore.

With great ceremony, I hung the sign on the Future Machine. Uncle Hector took a photo of me standing proudly in front of it, then I took a photo of Uncle Hector and Uncle Hodge doing the same, except Uncle Hodge gave the lamest of smiles and looked about as proud as a dead fieldmouse.

I said nothing. We began making plans for our trip back to Rev City.

"Someone will have to mind the store," said Uncle Hector.

We both looked at Uncle Hodge, who shrugged, as if to say, *Why not?* He didn't seem too bothered about missing out on another trip in the non-automatic sidecar.

"I'll show you what to do," I said confidently.

I explained carefully about the prices and the money box and the security camera which was really a shoebox and a broken telescope. Uncle Hodge stared blankly at the counter and scratched his head.

"Don't worry, Liam," whispered Uncle Hector. "The chances of Hodge getting a customer are a hundred to one. And the chances of him *selling* something are a zillion to one."

Uncle Hector turned his big alarming smile on Uncle Hodge and told him we wouldn't be long. Uncle Hodge smiled weakly back and edged into position behind the counter.

"OK, Liam," said Uncle Hector. "Let's teach that Rev City a lesson they'll never forget!"

We jumped on to the old Enfield and set off for town. Uncle Hector cried, "Yee-hah!" and dug his heels into the engine like a demented cowboy. The bike spluttered with the effort, but staggered forward like a faithful old dog. After a while, however, the engine got a bit hot, and Uncle Hector decided to stop in a field to let it cool down. We unpacked our sandwiches and sat on the grass, watching the old beast gently steaming.

"I hope it won't mind having to share a garage," I said.

"It won't have to," said Uncle Hector, munching on his favourite cheese-and-strawberry jam sandwich.

"Why's that?" I asked.

"We're getting rid of it," replied Uncle Hector. He tried to sound cool about this but I noticed he turned his face away from the old Enfield as he spoke.

"Why?" I asked, slightly shocked.

"I'm a 'one-bike man'," replied Uncle Hector. "Besides, we can't afford petrol for two."

"But ..." I began, "it's history!"

Uncle Hector took another munch of his sandwich.

"What will happen to it?" I asked.

Uncle Hector shrugged.

"Have you told Uncle Hodge?" I asked.

Uncle Hector nodded.

"What did Uncle Hodge say?" I asked.

"Do you know," said Uncle Hector, "I really can't remember." And before I could ask any more questions he leapt to his feet and told me it was time to *do the business*.

Chapter 10

A Small Success and a Big Disaster

....

Uncle Hector couldn't keep the smile off his face as we waltzed into Rev City. Then again, as I have said, Uncle Hector always had a smile on his face. But this really was a big one. It stretched from ear to ear and immediately caught the attention of Mr Merriman, Junior Sales Assistant.

"Back again, sir?" he said, with a sly smirk. "Perhaps I could interest you in a little moped."

"Oh no," replied Uncle Hector. "I want the Farley-Davidson Future Machine."

We marched across to the supersonic bike, with Mr Merriman scurrying to keep up.

"Yes, this is the one," announced Uncle Hector. "But I have seen it cheaper in another shop."

Mr Merriman was not worried. "As you

know, sir," he said, "we will match any price. How much was the bike in this other shop?"

"Ten pence," replied Uncle Hector.

Mr Merriman gave a little laugh. "Ten pence?" he repeated.

"Ten pence," replied Uncle Hector.

Mr Merriman's eyes narrowed. "And the name of this shop?" he asked.

"The Two Uncles General Stores," replied Uncle Hector.

"Two Uncles General Stores?" said the salesman. "That's a new one on me."

"I will take you there," replied Uncle Hector.

By now Mr Merriman wasn't sure what to do. He decided to fetch the Senior Salesman, who went to fetch the Junior Manager, who thought it best to fetch the Senior Manager. All four of them trooped out of the shop and got into a car to follow us.

All the way back I pictured myself rolling into school on the Future Machine, and everyone falling over backwards to be my friend and do my homework for me. The whole plan was working like clockwork. But as we turned into Uncle Hector's road, we were met by a surprising and slightly alarming sight. Uncle Hodge was in the middle of the road, dancing in a little circle, both hands knocking crazily on the sky like it was a great blue door. The moment he heard the Enfield, he stopped this strange behaviour and rushed to meet us like a lovesick puppy.

"I've ... I've ... sold something!" he spluttered.

"Well done, Hodge!" said Uncle Hector, climbing off the old Enfield.

"Was it the stuffed owl?" I asked.

Uncle Hodge shook his head.

"The tin bath?"

Uncle Hodge gave the thumbs down.

"The broken armchair?"

Uncle Hodge said no.

"We give in," said Uncle Hector. "What have you sold?"

A joyful smile spread across Uncle Hodge's face. He held up a pale wrinkly hand, shaking with excitement. Between thumb and forefinger was a shiny new ten pence piece.

Uncle Hector looked at me. I looked at Uncle Hector.

"Hodge," said Uncle Hector quietly. "You wouldn't, by any chance, have sold the *motor bike*, would you?"

Uncle Hodge's joyful smile grew into a great cheesy grin.

"Shall I put the old Enfield back in the garage?" he trilled.

Uncle Hector slumped slowly to the ground until his forehead was resting on the pavement. Moans and whimpers came from his throat and his left hand beat firmly and steadily on the road. I was quite sorry for Uncle Hector but a lot more sorry for myself. After all, I would soon be going in for an operation, with Chief Sister Nursie as head surgeon.

Uncle Hodge, meanwhile, was full of

confidence. Now that his luck was in he was trying his hardest to sell the stuffed owl to the four salesmen from Rev City. Even when they bolted for their car and disappeared in a squeal of tyres, he refused to give up.

At this point I noticed a humming noise, far away.

"Is that bees?" I asked.

The noise got louder. Uncle Hector looked up from the pavement. "Could it be lawnmowers?" he suggested.

The noise got louder still.

"It might be tractors," I said.

"Or motor bikes," said Uncle Hector.

My mouth dried. Hell's Nurses!

I shook hands warmly with Uncle Hector and thanked him for having me. Then I made a rapid tour of the house, picked up my belongings and said a short but sorry farewell to my beloved General Stores. With a final wave to Uncle Hodge, I promised a postcard and ran for my life. It seemed so sad to say goodbye like this, but I was rather keen to stay alive.

Just as I reached the end of the road, the fearsome tribe of nurses appeared at the other end. They'd spotted me for sure.

I had no idea my legs could move quite so fast, but unfortunately they had no idea where they were going. Then I spotted a sign which said "Station" and decided immediately to go for it. I flew down Station Road with my trousers coming down and my breakfast coming up. With a grateful heave I flung open the station door and rushed straight on to the platform without even bothering to buy a ticket. My luck was in. A train was waiting. But even as I climbed on board the sound of revving bikes came up loud and clear.

"Move!" I cried.

The train seemed to hear me and not a moment too soon. As the brakes eased and the engine came to life, the first of the Hell's Nurses came roaring on to the platform, followed by half a dozen others. I waved a

cheerful goodbye and they cursed and spat
and stamped with their great black boots.

I sank back into my seat and relaxed.
Surely I was safe now. But just as I began to
admire the scenery, I had a terrible shock.
Another dozen Hell's Nurses were racing
alongside the train, whirling stethoscopes
above their heads, like something out of an
old western. As we picked up speed, so did
they, fearless of any danger. Their nurses'
capes streamed behind them in the wind like
the wings of giant bats. One or two went
down into ditches as if shot, but the rest kept
right on coming, with their eyes firmly fixed
on my carriage.

Suddenly, up ahead, I saw a frightening
sight. Two of the bikes were towing an old
hospital bed, with the patient still sitting on
it, clutching the sheets and looking very
alarmed. Without warning the two bikes
turned towards the track, jumped it in one,
and left the bed stranded across the rails.
There was a squeal of breaks, then slowly we

came to a dead stop. The Hell's Nurses swarmed on to the side of the train like wasps on a jampot.

I had no choice. My only chance was to open a door and jump for it.

So that's what I did. I leapt for my life, rolled down the bank, then began scrambling madly up the other side, grabbing fistfuls of weeds and bushes to drag myself upwards.

But I had made a terrible mistake. At the top of the bank was a wire mesh fence, at least three metres high.

I reached the fence and began to climb like a demented monkey. The Hell's Nurses were right behind me. One mistake and I was done for.

Suddenly my foot slipped. My leg went dangling down like a loose bit of rope. In an instant it was seized. I tumbled to the ground and rolled into a ball with my eyes tight shut.

"Hello, Liam," said a familiar and surprisingly friendly voice.

I opened one eye. Chief Sister Nursie was standing over me. She was smiling.

"A-a-are you going to operate on me?" I stammered.

"Why?" asked Chief Sister Nursie.

"For losing your bike," I whimpered.

"What do you mean?" asked Chief Sister Nursie. "My bike's over there."

Chief Sister Nursie pointed to where the train had stopped. Sure enough, there stood a Farley-Davidson Future Machine, in perfect condition.

"I went to visit you," said Chief Sister Nursie. "I saw the bike there, so I decided to pick it up early. There was a strange little man there who insisted I gave him ten pence."

Gradually the mists cleared and I began to make sense of things. "*You* took the bike?" I asked.

"Who else?" replied Chief Sister Nursie.

Now I was really puzzled. "Then why are you chasing me?" I asked.

Chief Sister Nursie reached into her apron and drew out an empty jar of *Blue Lagoony*. "Can you get us some more of this stuff?" she asked.

Chapter 11

Victory!

....

I think Mum and Dad were expecting me home early. But I don't think they were expecting me to be riding pillion behind Chief Sister Nursie with an honour guard of fifty Hell's Nurses. The neighbours seemed quite surprised as well. They were used to the milkman, or maybe a taxi, but not a thundering cavalcade of piston-pumping motor bikes.

"Yo, Mum and Dad," I said, jumping down. "How's it hanging?"

Mum and Dad looked me up and down with their mouths open.

"Wicked holiday," I said.

Mum and Dad still couldn't bring themselves to speak.

"No time to waste," I said. "Better set up shop." With that I marched into the house, returning with my "Liam's Bygones" sign.

Mum and Dad watched with mounting horror as this was followed by my desk, various second-hand bargains and every jar of *Blue Lagoony* I could lay my hands on. Meanwhile, the Hell's Nurses formed an orderly queue, and all the way up the street curtains tweaked and faces poked out of doors.

Soon it was opening time, and my cash box was filling rapidly. I found something cheerful to say to every customer, about the weather, or the price of cheese, or the top speed of a Wakasaki 900.

In no time, it seemed, I was down to my last few jars of *Blue Lagoony*. Several neighbours had joined the queue, which now stretched right down the street and into the next street as well. I'm not sure if the neighbours knew what they were queuing for, but whatever it was, they didn't want to miss out.

At last the queue dwindled and the shop emptied. I even managed to sell the paintbrush and the china cat (one ear). The shoppers were in a kind of frenzy which only ended when Chief Sister Nursie and the Hell's Nurses rode off into the sunset, reeking of *Blue Lagoony*. They could probably smell it at the Bad Drains Department of the Council. No one complained, however. Somehow everyone was convinced it was the most beautiful smell in the world. I always thought it was, of course.

Quietly contented, I went back inside to count the takings and search for Mum and Dad. They didn't seem to be anywhere. Then, by chance, I looked out of the back window. There was Dad desperately picking rose petals while Mum collected them in a big bucket. Hmm, I thought. I wonder if I should give them the recipe. I wouldn't want them making something disgusting.

A few weeks later, just as I was getting ready for school, I heard the sound of an engine revving outside the house. I recognized it instantly. With a leaping heart, I threw open the curtains to see the dear old Enfield, with

Uncle Hodge at the helm and Uncle Hector riding pillion. The old bike shone in the sun and looked fifty years younger. So, for that matter, did my two uncles.

I rushed out to greet all three of them.

"Uncle Hodge!" I said. "Uncle Hector! What are you two doing here?"

"Taking you to school, of course!" replied Uncle Hodge.

"Just like we promised!" added Uncle Hector.

Fantastic, I thought. Then a small worry came to my mind.

"Hold on," I said. "If you're on the front, Uncle Hodge, and you're on the back, Uncle Hector ... where exactly do I go?"

Uncle Hodge and Uncle Hector both turned their eyes to the patch of space at the side of the old Enfield.

"On second thoughts," I said, "I think I'll catch the bus."

*   *   *